I CAN FLY

BY **RUTH KRAUSS**

ILLUSTRATED BY **MARY BLAIR**

 A GOLDEN BOOK • NEW YORK

Copyright © 1951, 1958, renewed 1979, 1986 by Penguin Random House LLC.
All rights reserved. Published in the United States by Golden Books, an imprint of Random House
Children's Books, a division of Penguin Random House LLC, 1745 Broadway, New York, NY 10019,
and in Canada by Penguin Random House Canada Limited, Toronto. Originally published in 1951
by Simon and Schuster, Inc., and Artists and Writers Guild, Inc. Golden Books, A Golden Book, A
Little Golden Book, the G colophon, and the distinctive gold spine are registered trademarks of Penguin
Random House LLC. A Little Golden Book Classic is a trademark of Penguin Random House LLC.
randomhousekids.com
Educators and librarians, for a variety of teaching tools, visit us at
RHTeachersLibrarians.com
Library of Congress Control Number: 91-077808
ISBN 978-0-307-00146-7 (trade) — ISBN 978-0-307-98276-6 (ebook)
A Bank Street Book
This book was originally published in 1951 in collaboration with the Bank Street College of Education,
an innovator in research in education for young children.
MANUFACTURED IN CHINA

A bird can fly.
So can I.

A cow can moo.

I can too.

I'm merrier

than a terrier.

Swish!

I'm a fish.

Pick pick pick

I'm a little chick.

My house is

like a mouse's.

A clam

is what I am.

Bump bump bump

I'm a camel with a hump.

Pitter pitter pat

I can walk like a cat.

Howl howl howl

I'm an old screech owl.

Gubble gubble gubble
I'm a mubble in a pubble.
I can play
I'm anything that's anything.
That's MY way.

I CAN FLY

Words by Hilda Marx

Music by Alec Wilder

Gayly

mf

I can fly like a bird, I can swim like a fish, I can grab like a crab, I can be what I wish.

Just by pre-tend-ing all through the day, I can be an-y-thing

I want to play — That's my way.

a tempo